Beatrice More and the Perfect Party

Beatrice More and the Perfect Party

Alison Hughes

ILLUSTRATED BY
Helen Flook

orca Echoes

ORCA BOOK PUBLISHERS

Library and Archives Canada Cataloguing in Publication

Hughes, Alison, 1966–, author
Beatrice More and the perfect party / Alison Hughes; illustrated by Helen Flook.
(Orca echoes)

Issued in print and electronic formats.
ISBN 978-1-4598-1709-8 (softcover).—ISBN 978-1-4598-1710-4 (PDF).—
ISBN 978-1-4598-1711-1 (EPUB)

I. Flook, Helen, illustrator II. Title. III. Series: Orca echoes

PS8615.U3165B42 2019   jc813'.6   C2018-904689-9
C2018-904690-2

Simultaneously published in Canada and the United States in 2019
Library of Congress Control Number: 2018954110

Summary: In this illustrated early chapter book, Beatrice plans a spectacular party for her little
sister, inspite of her family's attempts to help.

Orca Book Publishers gratefully acknowledges the support for its publishing
programs provided by the following agencies: the Government of Canada,
the Canada Council for the Arts and the Province of British Columbia through
the BC Arts Council and the Book Publishing Tax Credit.

Cover artwork and interior illustrations by Helen Flook
Edited by Liz Kemp
Author photo by Barbara Heintzman

ORCA BOOK PUBLISHERS
orcabook.com

Printed and bound in Canada.

22 21 20 19 • 4 3 2 1

For my children, for not caring that their parties were never perfect

—AH

CHAPTER ONE

The Calendar

Beatrice was sitting at her desk, making a list. The list was called *The List of Lists I Need to Make*.

She had a stack of paper and all her list-making supplies handy: a ruler (for underlining), a blue pen (for regular list items), a red pen (for special ones) and a stapler (because her lists often ran over many pages).

She had already written:

1

1. How to Deal with Possible Frustrations in Third Grade (e.g., gunky water fountains, classmates who chew with their mouths open, messy coat/boot areas, etc.)

2. Things That Need to Be Organized (e.g., the spice cupboard, the front closet, my thoughts and dreams, etc.)

3. Ways My Lazy Dog, Edison, Can Get More Exercise (e.g., fun games, use of whistles, any kind of treat, etc.)

4. The Many, Many Ways I Need to Help My Little Sister Get Ready for Kindergarten (e.g., practicing reading and spelling, using a hairbrush, avoiding being weird, etc.)

5. Important Things Happening in July and How to Prepare for Them

Beatrice paused. Today was June 30. They had moved into their new house only two weeks earlier. It seemed like longer than that. She had already made two good friends in the neighborhood—Sue and Jill. Beatrice had gotten her family unpacked and organized the very first day they moved in. But she noticed that the house was slowly getting messy again.

There was no getting around it—her family was simply never going to be as neat or as professional as she was.

Beatrice looked around her room and smiled with relief. No mess here. Her room was perfectly tidy and organized.

What is happening next month? she wondered. She reached for the calendar and flipped the page to July. Only one date, Saturday, July 14, was neatly circled twice in red pen.

Beatrice was shocked.

"Sophie's birthday! How could I have forgotten? I usually start planning

birthday parties months in advance! This move has put me off schedule."

Beatrice ran out of her room. There was no time to lose. She had to start planning this minute, this *second*! But where was Sophie? The planning had to be a secret. She wanted Sophie's party to be a surprise.

Beatrice tiptoed quietly across the hall to Sophie's room and put her ear to the door. She heard Sophie talking to her favorite toy, Mrs. Cow, who was actually a crabby-looking doll, not a cow.

"We *gots* to ride this stuffed frog because we got no *horse*, that's why, Mrs. Cow!" Sophie explained. Then there was a huge crash. Beatrice jumped, then knocked at the door.

"Sophie? Sophie? Are you okay?"

"I'N OKAY, BEE!" Sophie yelled. "YOU CAN'T RIDE A FROG WITHOUT HIM BEING A SLIPPERY LITTLE SUCKER SOMETIMES, YOU KNOW! WANNA RIDE?"

"Uh, maybe later," said Beatrice. She ran downstairs to find her mother.

CHAPTER TWO
The Planners

Beatrice found her mother in the kitchen, taking something burned out of the oven.

"Hi, Bee," she said cheerfully. "Want a square? They're ready to go. A teensy bit overdone maybe. But I'm sure we could chip them out of the pan—"

"Mom, we need to plan Sophie's birthday party," Beatrice exclaimed. "It's in two weeks. *Less* than two weeks,

7

if you don't count today and you don't count the actual day! Twelve days!"

"Gosh," said her mother, "you're right!" She chipped at the squares. Small burned pieces flew into the air. Their dog, Edison, gobbled them up as they fell and then licked the floor just to make sure. His tail wagged at this fun game.

"Anyway," said Beatrice's mother, "seeing as we don't know many people yet, maybe we should just have a family party for Sophie. Something simple."

Beatrice took a deep breath. "Mom," she said in a quiet voice, "Sophie is the best sister in the whole world. I have a long list that proves this!" She didn't mention that Sophie was also on her list of *People Who Make Me Feel Like Exploding*, because everyone was on that.

"She deserves a spectacular party, a *perfect* party!"

"Well, who am I to argue with one of your lists?" Her mother smiled, but she looked a little worried. "What do you have in mind, Bee?"

"I brought down a list I made several months ago. It's called *Fantastic Birthday Party Ideas.*"

"Uh, okay, let's hear it," said her mother.

"Number one is *Shuttle to the Moon*. That would indeed be fantastic," Beatrice said, "but it probably would take more than twelve days to arrange."

"Probably."

Beatrice ran her finger down the list. "*Deep Sea Diving?*"

Her mom shook her head. "No sea around, Bee, deep or otherwise."

"Hmmm. So, I guess *Luxury Cruise* is out too?"

"Let's think a little bit smaller," suggested her mom.

"*Hot Air Balloon Ride? Skydiving? Horse-Drawn Carriage? Private Circus? A Room Full of Puppies?*"

Fantastic Birthday Ideas
1 Shuttle to the Moon
2 Deep Sea Diving
3 Luxury Cruise
4 Hot Air Balloon Ride
5 Skydiving
6 Horse-Drawn Carriage
7 Private Circus
8 Puppy Room

"Even smaller, Bee. You know Sophie. She likes little things. Simple things. She'll be happy with a regular birthday party." She saw Beatrice's face and said quickly, "And by regular, I of course mean an extra-special birthday party, with all the usual birthday things."

"Well, *obviously* it'll be a surprise party with decorations, cake, balloons, games and prizes, right? Right?"

"Absolutely," Beatrice's mom said, looking relieved. "That sounds great. I'll make one of my famous birthday cakes!" Her mother chipped more burned squares out of the pan.

Beatrice opened her mouth, then closed it again. She swallowed. Her mother's birthday cakes *were* famous— famous for being lumpy, burned messes. But she put a lot of love into baking them, and Beatrice felt a little sorry for her that they were never successful.

"Excellent," Beatrice said bravely. "Now we have to have a theme. You can't have a party without a theme. What should it be? Magic? Cats? Soccer? And a color. We'll have to get matching decorations in Sophie's favorite color."

Beatrice paused. Her own favorite color was purple. Everyone knew that. But Sophie's?

"What's Sophie's favorite color, Mom?"

"Hmmm. I'm not sure," said her mother. "I don't think she's ever picked one."

"Everyone has a favorite color. I'll find Sophie and do some research," said Beatrice.

There was a crash in the living room.

Beatrice and her mom looked at each other.

"Sophie?" called her mom.

There was a loud *thunk, thunk, thunk*.

"It's okay, everboddy!" Sophie yelled. "That big crash wasn't actually my *body*! Or even my *head*!"

Beatrice closed her eyes.

"Okay, I'll go find out about her favorite color and what she wants for her birthday," said Beatrice.

"And I'll look for a new cake recipe!" Beatrice and her mother high-fived.

"Party planners on the job," Beatrice said. Her mother winked.

CHAPTER THREE

The Research

Beatrice found Sophie at the bottom of the stairs, stuffing toys back into a garbage bag.

"I chucked my bag of toys down the stairs and it *essploded*," she explained.

"*Ex*ploded," corrected Beatrice.

"Ex-essploded," said Sophie. "Good thing I thunked those down *personally*." She pointed to another bag filled with books.

Beatrice helped Sophie pick up toys.

"Why do you always bring so much stuff with you, Sophie?" Beatrice asked. Her little sister always messed up every room she played in.

Sophie shrugged. "Makes it cozy. I like my stuffies. And my books."

Beatrice remembered that she was supposed to be finding out Sophie's favorite color and what she wanted for her birthday.

"What toys do you like most of all?" she asked.

"Oh, all kinds o' stuff."

"But what kinds of stuff?"

"*Big* stuff. And little teeny stuff. Also stuff in the middle of those."

"No, what I mean is, what is your very favorite thing to play with?" Beatrice was trying to be patient.

"Mrs. Cow!" Sophie pointed to her crabby-looking baby doll. "Or Mr. Cow!" She hugged a ratty, worn yellow rabbit.

"Yes, yes, we all know about the Cows (who aren't cows at all). But how about something *other* than them?" said Beatrice, gritting her teeth.

"Super-Pig?" suggested Sophie, pointing at the goldfish in the bowl, which she had named.

Beatrice growled softly to herself.

"He's a fish, Sophie. A live fish."

"A *fun* fish!"

Beatrice stared over at the sluggish goldfish, who swam slowly in circles around and around his bowl. She would never have described Super-Pig as fun.

"I mean, what are your favorite *kinds* of toys. Building toys? Dolls? Crafts? Dress-up clothes? Stuffies? Models?"

"Yup. Those kinds. Hey, Bee!" Sophie said with a delighted laugh. "Your eye's doing that twitchy thing again. I *love* that twitchy little eye. Twitchy, twitchy, twitchums!"

Beatrice put up her hand to calm her eye.

"Let's talk about colors, Sophie. You draw and color a lot. You must have a *favorite* color. Mine's purple."

"Everboddy knows *that*, Bee."

"But what's *your* favorite color?"

Sophie rubbed up her fuzzy hair, thinking.

"Rainbow," she said finally.

"*Rrrr*, Sophie, rainbow is not a color!" Beatrice snapped. Then she remembered that Sophie was just little, and she took a deep breath. "A rainbow is a *group* of colors, Sophie!

Seven colors. Here's a sentence I use to remember the seven colors of the rainbow: Really Organized Young Girls are Brilliant, Imaginative and Very professional. See? Each letter stands for a color of the rainbow—Red, Orange, Yellow, Green, Blue, Indigo (which is a deep blue) and Violet. So out of all those colors, what *one color* in the rainbow is your very favorite?"

Sophie tapped her chin with one finger and squinted her eyes.

"Those are *all* my *very* favorite colors," said Sophie. "Plus black." She sat down in the middle of her mess of toys. "Hey, Bee, *my* sentence is going to be"—Sophie squinted her eyes—"Roosters cOck-a-doodle-doo Yelling Gorilla Babies In Velvety…blankets! Get it? That's how roosters *lullaby*. Baby gorillas, at least."

"Good sentence, Sophie," said Beatrice. *This has not been successful at all*, she thought.

Sophie grabbed one of her books off the floor. "I love books. Books and little baby gorillas."

Beatrice left Sophie and went upstairs to her room. She wrote a list of *Possible Presents for Sophie's Perfect Party*:

Big, teeny and in-between-sized stuff

Every toy Sophie already has (especially Mr. and Mrs. Cow)

Any other toy in the world

Another fish

Something with every color of the rainbow

A baby gorilla

Books

It was a weird list. Beatrice saw that right away. Still, she felt more professional having written it down on paper.

CHAPTER FOUR

The Guests

Beatrice, Jill and Sue walked to the park.

"So here's our mission," Beatrice said. "We need to find kids to invite to Sophie's birthday party. Any kids that are close to Sophie's age. I printed up thirty invitations. Mom says Sophie plays with kids at the park, so we need to find them, tell them about the party and make them promise to come!"

"Okay, Bee," said Sue through a mouthful of apple. "Bunch of little kids. Party. We're on it."

Beatrice scanned the playground, looking for small people. Scouting for possible party guests.

"I see some!" she said. "Come on, let's go!"

Beatrice ran up to a little girl who was heading for the swings.

"I got here first!" the little girl shrieked, grabbing the swing.

"I wasn't trying to take your swing, little girl," said Beatrice. "I'm inviting you to a fun party!" She smiled at the girl's mother. "Excuse me, but I was wondering if your little girl plays with my sister, Sophie. We're new here."

"Sophie? No, I don't—"

"She's super nice, and she can't

help her fuzzy, messy red hair," Beatrice explained.

"I'm sure she's sweet—"

"So will your daughter come to her birthday party? Saturday, July 14? Here's an invitation, and here is my business card, just so you know we're a *very* professional family."

"Uh..."

"Great!" said Beatrice. "See you there!"

"One guest already," she said to Jill. Beatrice squeezed Jill's arm excitedly.

"Wow, that was quick!" said Jill. "I've been trying to catch up with this little guy. He's fast, and now he thinks we're playing tag."

A little boy in a blue soccer shirt raced past and tapped Jill on the arm. "You're it!" he screamed and took off.

"This is hard work," Jill shouted over her shoulder. Beatrice was grateful for her speedy friend.

"Bee!" Sue called. "Over here. I got one!" Sue was hauling a grinning little girl across the playground. The little girl waved.

"Sue, maybe we better not actually pick them up," said Beatrice.

"Oh, it's okay. This is Kayley. I babysit this squirmy little squirt and her brother. Kyle's tearing around here somewhere. They live down the block."

"Hi, Kayley! Great job, Sue! *Two* more guests!"

"Just letting you know that Kayley eats a *lot*—"

"There's going to be cake, right?" Kayley demanded. "*Lots* of cake?"

"Oh, yes, a beautiful, big, perfectly

baked cake," Beatrice said. *At least I hope that's what it is*, she thought.

"And Kyle talks. A *lot*," said Sue. "Here he comes now."

"Hey, why does Kayley get a ride, Sue?" a little boy with spiky hair said. "*I* want a ride. I want exactly as long a ride as Kayley got, and then maybe even a little bit *more* of a ride because I'm a little bit older and I should get—"

Kayley started screaming in protest.

Beatrice wondered if Sophie would actually want these two at her party. But a party needed guests, so she handed them each an invitation.

Kyle and Kayley were giving her a headache, so she went and handed out invitations to all the parents standing around the playground.

She noticed a quiet little girl playing

by herself in the sand. Her brown hair was even messier than Sophie's.

Doesn't anyone brush their hair? Beatrice wondered. The little girl hummed to herself as she shoved sand into a giant pile.

"You don't happen to know my sister, Sophie, do you?" asked Beatrice. "About your age, messy red hair, has a crabby baby doll."

"Mrs. Cow!" said the girl, with a big smile.

"That's her! You know her! Would you like to come to her birthday party?"

"Sure!" said the little girl. "I'm Annie."

"Well, Annie," said Beatrice, "here's an invitation! I hope you can make it. There will be tons of guests! It's going to be a fabulous surprise party!"

But as Beatrice turned away, she worried. Would it be a fabulous party? Would there be tons of guests? Would there be a big, beautiful cake?

Beatrice hoped she had not just lied to several small children.

CHAPTER FIVE

The Decorations

"They're somewhere in here," said her father. He was pulling out boxes from their basement storage room. "I bought a ton of decorations when that dollar store was closing out, remember, Bee?"

"The name's Beatrice, Dad. Not Bee. A bee is an insect with a stinger. Not a successful little girl."

"Ha ha, right you are, Bee." Her father's voice was muffled by the boxes.

"I always think Bee suits you. You know. Bee More. It's like a motto!"

Beatrice wasn't really listening. She looked around the basement and sighed. It had been so neat and tidy when they moved in just a couple of weeks ago. Now it was a mess. Good thing they were going to have Sophie's birthday party *outside*. Their backyard wasn't as messy as the house.

"Skates, books, tools, toys—wow! My old sports trophies!" Her father knocked over a box as he swung around. He held up a little trophy. "Won this baby when I was probably your age, Bee!"

Beatrice gritted her teeth. She counted to ten. Then she took a deep breath.

"Nice, Dad. Maybe we can look at your very old childhood trophies later. Better find those *decorations*, right?"

"Gotcha!" her dad said. He dived back into the boxes. "Found it!" he finally called, hauling out a box marked *Decorations*.

"Excellent, Dad!" Bee said with relief.

Her father opened the box. He pulled out a banner with black, dripping letters that spelled out *Have a Howling Halloween!*

"Ha ha, well, guess we can't use that one," he said.

Beatrice grabbed the box. She dug deeper. There were three packages of paper plates with green shamrocks on them and the words *The Luck of the Irish!* There were heart-shaped *Be My Valentine!* balloons. There were reindeer-antler headbands and Santa hats. There were paper Thanksgiving turkeys. There were invitations to wedding showers.

There were cards saying *Thank You for the Baby Gift!*

But there were no birthday decorations.

Beatrice started to panic. She pawed through the box.

"Goblin masks? Seriously, Dad?" Beatrice shrieked, holding up an assortment of Halloween decorations. A fake eyeball fell from her hand, bounced on the floor and rolled into a corner. Edison, who had been snoozing on the couch, perked up his ears and ran after the eyeball like they were playing a fun game of fetch.

Her father was starting to look worried.

"Let me look," he said. "There's *got* to be some birthday things." He rummaged. "Aha!" He pulled out a crumpled blue plastic tablecloth. "Never been used!"

He also pulled out two bags of orange and black balloons, several packages of napkins with pink fish on them, some candles, purple party hats, paper plates and cups, and a big bag of noisemakers.

"Ta-dah!" he said. "We are ready to *party*!"

"Dad," Beatrice said, trying to calm her voice, which seemed to want to scream, "those are *Halloween* balloons. Those paper plates have farm animals on them. Those cups are decorated with some kind of swamp creature! And those noisemakers say *Happy New Year*!"

"Well, a birthday is a new year for the person having the birthday, right?" Her father stopped when he saw his daughter's face. "Look, Bee, Sophie loves animals."

"But Dad! Swamp creatures?" Beatrice wailed. "That looks like a frog, but what is *that*? Some kind of swamp dragon?"

"Heh heh. Pretty cool. Sophie won't care—she'll love this stuff," he said. "And it seems silly to spend money on more decorations when we have all we need right here. Wait! Here's a banner we can use!" He pulled out a long banner with green and red lettering.

"That says *Ho, Ho, Ho!*, Dad."

"Perfect! Sophie loves to laugh!"

Beatrice's shoulders sagged. She stuffed the odd assortment of decorations into a bag.

"I'll try to figure out some way to tie all these decorations together with a theme," she said bravely. What she didn't say was *so that this party doesn't look like the least professional birthday party EVER*. But that's how she felt.

"Thanks, Dad." Beatrice began to climb the stairs.

"No problem, Bee. I *knew* that stuff would come in handy." Her father smiled and waved at her.

His other hand was wrestling the Halloween eyeball out of Edison's drooly mouth.

CHAPTER SIX

The Idea

Sophie was coloring in the living room. Beatrice tiptoed past her with the bag of decorations and headed for the stairs.

"HOLD IT RIGHT THERE, MISSY!" yelled Sophie, pointing a purple crayon.

Beatrice froze. She turned slowly.

"There's nothing in this bag, Sophie," Beatrice said quickly. "Just a bunch of junk from the basement."

"What?" said Sophie, looking puzzled. "Oh, you thought I meant *you*, Bee?!" Sophie laughed. "I was talking to *Missy*!" She pointed her crayon at a tiny, ratty stuffed horse. I'n telling Missy there to stay *purvectly* still. I'n drawing her picture!"

"Ah," said Beatrice, relieved. Sophie held up the picture. It showed a horselike animal standing on top of a huge purple mountain.

"That's a nice picture, Sophie. Hey, you're drawing a *purple* mountain."

"Yeah, it's purply. Missy says she likes purple grass. It's yummy to eat."

Beatrice wondered whether Sophie had any normal toys. They all seemed to have weird names or do weird things.

"Do *you* like purple too, Sophie?"

"I love purple, silly. This picture's for *you*, Bee. You love purple. I love you, so I must love purple!"

"I love you too, Sophie," Beatrice said, giving Sophie a hug.

She didn't even try to smooth Sophie's tangled mess of hair.

She didn't even care that Sophie got a smear of purple crayon on her white shirt.

Sophie struggled out of the hug. "I gotta finish this. Missy won't stand still forever, you know!"

Beatrice grabbed the bag of decorations and ran up to her room.

After seeing the kind of decorations she had for the party, Beatrice was so depressed that she made up her mind to cross *Perfect Party Planner* off her list of *Very Professional Jobs to Consider*. But talking with Sophie had made her feel a bit better.

Maybe sometimes to be a very professional party planner, you have to

work with what you have to make a perfect party, she thought.

And Sophie had given her an idea.

Beatrice dumped out the bag of decorations.

She got out her box of craft supplies.

And she got to work.

CHAPTER SEVEN

The Gift

Beatrice and her mother wandered through the giant toy store.

"This is our third toy store," said her mother with a sigh. "The last one in town."

"Those other toy stores were lame," Beatrice said. "They just had ordinary toys. Average toys. No toy that is *absolutely perfect*." She scanned the shelves anxiously.

"Maybe we shouldn't be aiming for perfect," said her mother. "How about we shoot for fun or really good?"

Beatrice wasn't listening. They were in the last aisle of the toy store, and nothing seemed special enough. She started to panic.

"Gee, I think Sophie would love *any* of these things," said her mother, stifling a yawn. "How about this?" She held up a big dog puzzle. "She loves Edison."

"It's cute, but it's not super special."

"Okay, how about this?" Her mother held up an art set. "Sophie's always drawing and coloring!"

"Sophie already has a million crayons and markers. I'm always cleaning them up."

Her mother shoved the craft set back on the shelf.

"Oh, I know! A doll! Sophie likes dolls. *This* doll is way less crabby-looking than Mrs. Cow!" Her mother held out a doll hopefully.

"Yes, but Sophie *loves* Mrs. Cow, Mom. We can't just buy her another doll and say 'Here's a prettier, better dressed, way less crabby-looking doll, Sophie. Love *this*!'"

"Ooookay," said her mother. She slumped down on a little-kids' bench and eased off her shoes. "I'm just going to look for toys from here."

Beatrice was trotting down the aisle, looking left and right. Nothing.

There has to be a really, really special gift that will make up for the weird party decorations and the probably burned birthday cake, Beatrice thought frantically.

She came to the end of the aisle,
ran around the corner and collided with
someone.

"Oh, sorry," she said. But the someone
turned out to be a some*thing*—a toy, not
a person. Beatrice looked closer. The big
furry thing was a horse. A sturdy horse
that a child could ride on. It was striped
with all the colors of the rainbow. It had
a fun little saddle and some reins to hold.
It had happy brown eyes and a stuffed

carrot stitched to its big, smiling teeth. It had shiny black hooves. Beatrice looked at the horse's name tag. It said *Patty, the Party Pony.*

Beatrice remembered Sophie crashing around in her room, trying to ride her "slippery little sucker" frog because she had no horse! She remembered Missy, Sophie's tiny, shabby horse, being drawn on the purple mountain in her picture. She remembered all the horse pictures Sophie had drawn. And she remembered how Sophie said that she loved *all* the colors of the rainbow.

This was it! This horse, Patty the Party Pony, was Sophie's perfect present!

"Mom! Mom! Momomomomom!" Beatrice yelled, grabbing the horse by the neck and dragging it around the corner.

Her mother struggled to her feet.

"What? What is it, Bee? What's *that*???"

"I found it! Sophie's perfect present! Ta-daaaah!" Beatrice shoved the horse toward her mother. Beatrice was out of breath. "Her name is Patty, and she's a pony for parties! And Sophie loves horses! And she can stop riding a frog! Which is weird. And rainbow is her favorite color! Even though it's really seven colors."

"Sophie will absolutely *love* it," her mother agreed. She grabbed the horse and lugged it over to the checkout before Beatrice could change her mind. "Oof, this thing is *huge*!"

"Huge and perfect!" Beatrice skipped beside her mother, picking up the reins that were dragging on the floor.

"And we can go home now!" her mother said, sounding very glad.

Beatrice grabbed her mother and the horse in a tight hug.

Finally something about this party was absolutely perfect!

CHAPTER EIGHT

The Hiding Spot

The pony didn't fit in the car trunk, no matter how much Beatrice and her mother turned it and twisted it. So they drove home with it squashed beside Beatrice in the back seat. Its head and neck stuck out the window like a huge rainbow-colored dog's. The carrot in its mouth bounced in the breeze.

"Where should we hide Patty, Mom?" Beatrice was worried. "She has to be a surprise."

"Hmmm, I don't think that sucker will fit in any of the closets. How about behind some boxes in the basement?"

"Sophie is always making forts down there, and making a huge mess," said Beatrice, shaking her head. "No, it has to be a more private place. Hey! There *is* one private place! We can put it in my room."

"Good idea," said her mother. "Everybody stays out of your room.

Probably because you have a sign on the door that says *Everybody Stay <u>Out</u>!*"

"You let one person in, and the mess comes with them," said Beatrice, shrugging.

But what if she let one pony in? She swallowed nervously, trying to think where she could keep it without it crumpling her rug or blocking her closet or rumpling her bedspread.

They pulled into the driveway, and her mother ran to the door to see if Sophie and Dad were still at the park. She waved from the door.

"The coast is clear!" she called. "Need some help, Bee?"

"Mom," Beatrice said, "I'm *eight years old*. I think I can manage a little pony."

She wrestled the pony out of the car and up the two stairs to the front door.

But the pony got stuck in the doorway. Beatrice used all her strength to push the horse.

"This…horse…has…*very*…strong… legs," Beatrice said between gritted teeth.

She and the horse finally popped through the door, landing in a plushy heap.

"Okay, we're in," Beatrice sighed. She looked at the horse. It was still smiling, the carrot dangling from its mouth. "You're cute, Patty, but annoying," said Beatrice.

Bump, bump, bump. She dragged the horse stair by stair up to the second floor, where the bedrooms were. All the bumping woke Edison, who stretched and wandered over for a look at the huge, interesting creature Beatrice was playing with.

"Whew," Beatrice said when they reached the landing. She wiped her sweaty forehead. "Party planning is hard work. Okay, you just stay here, Patty"—she shoved the horse against the wall—"and I'll find a spot for you in my room."

She went into her room and looked around. It was perfectly neat and organized. Where could she put this thing? Not on the bed. She couldn't mess up all her carefully organized stuffies. They were lined up alphabetically by name. Over by the bookshelf? No. That was where she put her lists before filing them in boxes and then stacking the boxes neatly in her closet. The closet? No. There was no room, and it was all perfectly organized according to color anyway.

It would have to be in the middle of the room, in the middle of the purple rug.

Beatrice took a deep breath. It wouldn't mess up her room for long. The party was in a couple of days. It would be in Sophie's messy room by Saturday.

She ran out to get the horse.

She stopped.

"Aaaaaahhhhhh!" Beatrice shrieked.

Edison had knocked over the rainbow pony. He was happily chewing on one of its shiny hooves. Another hoof was chewed up as well. He looked at Beatrice and thumped his tail. A piece of shiny black hoof dropped from his mouth.

Beatrice grabbed the pony and pulled it away from Edison.

"Oh, Edison! Bad dog! Shoo!"

Edison slunk downstairs.

"What's the matter, Bee?" her mother called from the bottom of the stairs.

"Edison has *ruined* Sophie's perfect gift!" Beatrice was nearly in tears. "It is no longer a perfect rainbow pony. It is a chewed and drooly rainbow *mess*!"

"Oh dear," said her mother. "Maybe we can—"

But Beatrice wasn't listening. She was wrestling the pony into her room.

She dragged it right into the middle of her carpet.

She threw a big purple blanket over it. It didn't quite cover the chewed-up hooves.

Beatrice went over to her box of lists. She flipped to her list of *What To Do When I Feel Like Screaming*. She went down the list, past numbers one through seven (including such things as *take deep breaths*, *listen to soothing music* and *run frantically on the spot*), to number eight: *cover my head with my pillow and actually scream into my bed.*

That one seemed very appealing at the moment.

Beatrice reached for her pillow.

CHAPTER NINE

The Schedule

Beatrice sat at her desk.

Organization, she said to herself. *That's what this party needs. I can't do much about the decorations or the cake.* She swallowed nervously, thinking about the cake her mother was going to bake the next morning. *But I can make sure the party goes according to plan.*

She picked up a pencil and a ruler and made two columns on a sheet of paper.

Above the first column she wrote *Time*, and over the second, *Activity*.

She wrote:

Time	Activity
2pm EXACTLY	Guests arrive (smile, greet, chit-chat, etc)
2·03pm	Hustle guests into kitchen (drop off presents, chit-chat, give instructions)
2·04pm	Hand out hats and noisemakers (one set per person)
2·07pm	Get guests to hide for the big "SURPRISE!" shout when Dad brings Sophie back from library

Beatrice hesitated. She had told her dad that on Saturday, his job was to take Sophie to the library and bring her back at 2:15 *exactly*. But she wondered if he had really been listening. He had been watching baseball two of the three times she told him.

She ran downstairs to find him and tell him one more time.

"What party?" her father said. "*This* Saturday? Oh shoot, I'm busy." He saw Beatrice's face. "Joke. I was joking."

This family is really quite frustrating, she thought as she ran upstairs. But she didn't have time to add to her list of *Things That Are Frustrating*. It was one of her longest lists—seventeen pages at last count.

When she got upstairs, the door to her room was open.

What is going on? Everyone knows to stay out of my room!

Beatrice went in and saw something moving under the purple blanket she had thrown over Patty the Party Pony. She saw a brown, shaggy tail thumping in excitement.

"Edison!" she yelled.

The moving thing under the blanket stopped. The tail stopped too.

"Edison, come! Out! I can *see* your tail. I know you're there."

Beatrice sighed. She walked Edison two times every day. She fed him very healthy food. She worked on training him each day. But Edison didn't really listen. He only moved for treats.

"Want a treat, Edison?" She grabbed one from a jar on her desk and tossed it into the hallway.

Edison scrambled to his feet and tore after the treat, dragging the purple blanket off the pony.

Beatrice threw the blanket back over the pony just as she heard a small voice from the door.

"Wow, whatcha got there, Bee?" Sophie was standing there, holding Mrs. Cow by one foot.

Beatrice froze. She stalled. "What do I have where?" she said.

"There. The huge purple thing. Behind you, silly."

"Oh, *this*," said Beatrice. "This, Sophie…is a…it's a…"

"Is it a fort? No! It's a *mountain*!" Sophie's jaw dropped open. "A purple mountain! Just like the purple mountain in my *picture*! Did you make it *because* of my picture?"

"Yes," Beatrice said in relief. "I looked at your picture and—you guessed it—decided that I wanted my very own purple mountain. Right here in the center of my room." Beatrice patted the purple mound nervously. She noticed a chewed hoof sticking out and nudged it back under the blanket with her foot.

"Here." She grabbed another purple blanket from her bed. "Let's go to *your* room and make a purple mountain for *you*."

Sophie shrieked with delight and bundled up the blanket.

"C'mon, Bee! I gots to have one! My own purple mountain! Mrs. Cow! We gonna have our own *mountain*..." Sophie ran across the hall to her room.

That was a close one, Beatrice thought.

She followed Sophie, shutting her door very, very carefully.

CHAPTER TEN

The Big Day

It was Saturday, the day of the party.

"Dad," hissed Beatrice. "It's already noon! You have to get Sophie out of here so Mom and I can make the cake and decorate for the party!"

"Gotcha, Bee." Her father winked. He pulled on his baseball cap. "Hey, Sophie," he called into the kitchen. "Time to go to the library. Remember?"

"Nah," said Sophie, who was coloring at the kitchen table.

"But you love the library, Sophie," Bee said in a fake-cheerful voice.

"I do love the liberarry. But I'm busy." Sophie was scribbling with black marker. Beatrice winced as it marked the table.

"Well, you can take all your stuff with you and finish your picture at the library," said Beatrice, dumping the markers into Sophie's backpack. She shoved Mrs. Cow on top. "There! All set! Off you go! Have fun!"

"But—" said Sophie.

"Dad will buy you ice cream," said Beatrice quickly.

"Ice cream!"

"Yes, and he'll give you a piggyback ride the whole way there!"

"Yay!"

"Hey, that's hard on the old back," said her dad. But Beatrice was already lifting Sophie up onto his back.

Sophie giggled. "See ya, Bee! Giddyup, horsie!"

Beatrice waved. Then she slammed and locked the door.

"Mom!" Beatrice called. "Time to bake Sophie's cake!"

Her mother carried a big cookbook out of the kitchen.

"Got the recipe right here," she said. "Doesn't this look great?" She pointed to a picture. It showed a perfect, beautiful double-layer cake with blue icing.

"Wow, it sure does." Beatrice nodded. She felt guilty for wondering just how different her mother's cake would look.

"Now I'm not sure if you've ever noticed, Bee," said her mother, tossing a few cups of flour into a mixing bowl, "but sometimes I bake things just a *teensy* bit too long. But not this cake."

"Great, Mom." Beatrice felt relieved. Maybe this wouldn't be such a disaster after all. She watched her mother spill some sugar onto the floor. She watched her spoon eggshells out of the batter. "Uh, need some help?" Beatrice asked.

"Nope!" her mother said cheerfully. "I got this." As she mixed the batter around and around, bits of it flew everywhere. Edison ran around licking them up. "Why don't you decorate the backyard?"

"Good idea." Beatrice ran and got the box of decorations. On the way to the backyard, she tidied the living room. She cleaned the front closet.

She organized the back entrance. Finally she brought the box of decorations out to the backyard.

Dad had forgotten to mow the grass, she noticed. And Edison had dug several new holes.

"*Rrrrrr,*" said Beatrice.

She put the blue plastic tablecloth on the picnic table, taping it in place so it didn't blow off. She blew up all the balloons.

"Black and orange," she muttered. "Happy Halloween."

She stacked thirty plates, thirty party hats and thirty napkins. She set out the Toss the Beanbag into the Swamp Creature's Mouth game she had made. She taped a plastic donkey on the fence for Pin the Tail on the Donkey. She used chalk to carefully mark the start and finish lines for the sack race. She filled up a big bucket with water for a fishing game. She taped a large copy of her party schedule to the fence.

Finally she pasted up the banner. She had covered up the *Ho, Ho, Ho!* by gluing on big, fun purple letters that said *Welcome to Sophie's Awesome Animal Party!* It was the only theme she could think of that included swamp creatures, farm animals, fish and ponies.

When Beatrice was done, she looked around the yard. It was ready for a party. A weird and mismatched party, but still—a party.

Time check, she thought. She went into the house. The clock in the hall said it was 1:30 PM.

Half an hour until everybody gets here, she thought, feeling a little nervous.

She ran into the kitchen.

"The two parts of the cake are cooling, Bee," said her mother. She was mixing a big bowl of icing. "I didn't burn them! I took them out ten minutes early, just to be sure."

Ten minutes early? Beatrice would rather her mom had followed the recipe exactly. Cookbooks were written by highly professional cake-making people.

"Almost ready to stack them and cover them with icing!" her mother said. "How do they feel? Cool?"

Beatrice looked at the two round cakes. They were not burned. They were the opposite of burned. They were so not-burned that each cake had sunk right down in the middle into a mushy, sunken mess.

"Hmmm," said Beatrice, trying not to panic. "Yes, I believe they are cool."

"Well, let's slap some of this icing—" Her mother turned and stared at the sunken cakes. "Oh no! What *happened* to them? They were fine when I took them out of the oven!"

Beatrice looked at the clock. They had only fifteen minutes before the guests would be arriving. There was no time to make another cake.

She felt her left eye start to twitch.

She felt frustration bubble up.

This party is going to be a total disaster, she thought.

"I'm sorry, Bee," her mother said. Her shoulders slumped, and she looked near tears. "You wanted everything to be just perfect."

"It's okay, Mom." Beatrice patted her mother's shoulder. Her mother had tried her best. She tried to think of what she could say to make her feel better.

Beatrice had an idea. Her eye stopped twitching.

"Mom," she said urgently, "you made blue icing, right?"

"Right." Her mother held out the bowl. "Tons of it."

"Do you have any *red* food coloring?"

Her mother rummaged in the cupboard. She held out a small container.

"I don't know how this is going to fix this mess of a cake," she said.

"It's not going to *be* a cake, Mom! It's going to be a *mountain*! A purple mountain! There's no time to explain, but Sophie will absolutely *love* it!"

Her mother laughed and hugged Beatrice. "Then let's make a mountain!"

Beatrice added drops of red food coloring to the blue icing. As she stirred, the icing turned purple.

"Perfect!" she said. They turned to the collapsed cakes. The cakes fell apart as they took them out of the pans.

"Doesn't matter," muttered Beatrice. "The icing will hold it all together."

They piled pieces of cake into the shape of a mountain. Then both of them took butter knives and slathered the mountain with purple icing, up and down and around and around.

"Well, this is a lovely purple mountain," said her mother, standing back to admire it.

Beatrice put five candles in a circle right at the top.

"It's great, Mom!" said Beatrice. "Just like Sophie's picture!"

They high-fived as the doorbell rang.

CHAPTER ELEVEN

The Party

The first birthday guest was Annie, the little girl with the messy hair.

"Hi, Annie! Thanks for coming." Beatrice smiled at her. She looked past Annie and her mother to see if any other children were coming up the walk. There was nobody else in sight.

Annie's mother came in and talked to Beatrice's mother. Beatrice explained to Annie that when the other kids arrived, they were all going to hide and, when Sophie got home, jump out and yell, "Surprise!"

But where were all the other kids? Beatrice was worried.

She checked the door several times.

She looked up and down the street.

The seconds ticked into minutes, and by 2:11 Beatrice's heart was pounding.

"Mom, this is horrible!" she whispered. "Who ever heard of a birthday party with one guest?"

"There's also *us*," said her mother, smiling. "And Annie's mother. That's *five*."

The doorbell rang, and Beatrice sprinted over and flung it open. Her friends Jill and Sue stood there.

"Hiya, Bee," said Sue. "Those little stinkers Kayley and Kyle couldn't come to the party, so we thought we'd come instead."

"Yeah, Sophie's our friend too," said Jill. "We brought gifts!"

"We brought Jimbo too," said Sue, dragging Jill's twin brother up the stairs. James had glasses and very neat hair.

"James. The name is *James*, Sue. Hello, Beatrice," he said. "My gift for Sophie is a brush. To help with her hair."

"That is a very thoughtful gift, James," Beatrice said.

James was Beatrice's main competition to be the smartest, most successful kid in third grade. But Beatrice didn't have time to worry that this party would look totally unprofessional to James.

She turned to Jill and Sue. "Thank you so much for coming!"

"Bee," her mother called from across the room. She pointed urgently at the clock.

"Quick, quick!" said Beatrice. She shooed Sue, Jill and James into the kitchen. "Sophie will be here in a minute! Grab a noisemaker! We have to hide!"

"What is that purple hill thing?" asked James, pointing at Sophie's birthday cake.

"It's not a *hill*—it's a *mountain*. Obviously," said Beatrice. "Go hide."

Everyone scattered into the living room and hid.

They waited.

The clock ticked.

Any second now, thought Beatrice, ready to spring up and shout, "Surprise!" But where was Dad? Where was Sophie?

Somebody slipped behind the sofa with her.

"This is fun!" Sophie whispered in Beatrice's ear. "Why are we hiding, Bee?"

"*Sophie*!" Beatrice jumped. "What are you doing here?"

"I *live* here, Silly-Billy!" Sophie laughed delightedly.

"No, I mean, how did you get in here?"

"Oh, Dad was talking and talking with Mr. Tan next door, an' so I just comed home. Did you know there's *balloons* in the backyard, Bee?"

"Oh, this is ridiculous," said Beatrice, getting to her feet. "Everybody, Sophie's right *here*." Heads popped up from behind furniture.

"Surprise!" everyone yelled at different times.

"*Phhhwwwt.*" Sue blew a lonely blast on her noisemaker, then waved.

"Surprise!" Sophie yelled too, clapping her hands.

The front door flew open.

"Surprise!" shouted Beatrice's dad. "Looks like you got to your party right on time, Sophie!" He looked nervously at Beatrice.

"*My* party?" said Sophie, sounding amazed.

Annie ran up to Sophie. "Happy birthday, Sophie!"

"It's my birthday!" Sophie said, hugging her. "I forgot what day it was!"

Everyone went out tow the backyard and put on party hats. Beatrice's father put on Sophie's favorite music.

"Animal plates! And swamp guys!" Sophie said, admiring the decorations on the cups. "And fishy napkins! I gots to keep one to show our fish, Super-Pig. He'll be *very* interested."

Beatrice lugged Patty the Party Pony down from her room. *We're not keeping to the party schedule at all*, she thought worriedly.

"Light the candles, Mom, and bring out the cake!"

Her mother lit the candles and carefully carried the cake out into the backyard.

"And Sophie, here's a special purple-mountain cake, which Beatrice says you'll love, for some reason," said her mother.

"A purply mountain!" shrieked Sophie, her eyes wide. "That's the best cake I ever seen! It's ezzactly like my picture!" Sophie happily swiped a finger down the side of the mountain and licked purple icing.

"And here's a rainbow horse to go with it!" called Beatrice. Her face was red as she dragged the pony outside and plunked it down in front of Sophie. The longish grass hid the horse's chewed-up hooves.

Sophie's mouth fell open.

"I can actually *ride* on that sucker?" she whispered, pointing to the saddle.

"Absolutely," said Beatrice. "And Mrs. Cow can too!"

Sophie stroked the rainbow horse, smearing purple icing on its head.

"I hope you like it, Sophie. I wanted you to have a fun party. A perfect party," said Beatrice.

Sophie ran and launched herself into Beatrice's arms in one of her flying monster hugs.

"It's great! All my best friends! And a purply mountain cake! And a rainbow horse! My favorite color!"

"*Seven* colors, remember?" said Beatrice. "Red, orange...oh, whatever. Her name is Patty the Party Pony. Isn't that pretty? It says so right here on the tag!"

"But that's not his *real* name," said Sophie, laughing. "That's just a *store* name. I'n gonna call him..." She tilted her bushy red head and tapped a finger on her chin, thinking. "Stompin' Jones!"

Stompin' Jones? Beatrice shrugged. Sophie was happy. It was her birthday. It was her horse. She could name it something weird and unprofessional if she wanted to.

Beatrice smiled as she watched Sophie and Mrs. Cow scramble up into the horse's saddle. And even though the party was nothing like the perfect party she had planned, she couldn't stop smiling.

She smiled as she watched Sue passing out balloons and Jill putting a party hat on Edison.

She smiled at James, whose hair got messed up as he lifted Annie up onto the horse, behind Sophie.

She smiled at her tired-looking mother, who was sprawled in a lawn chair, laughing with Annie's mother, who sat beside her. She smiled at her father, who was cutting the purple mountain with his purple party hat sitting crooked on his head.

She smiled at Sophie, who was riding her horse and shrieking with laughter. Sophie waved at Beatrice with a hand stained with purple icing.

"Hey, Bee!" screamed Sophie. "This party is absolutely *purvect*!"

ALISON HUGHES writes for children of all ages. Her books have been nominated for many awards, including the Governor General's Literary Award. She shares her love of writing by giving lively presentations and workshops at schools and young-author conferences. She lives in Edmonton, Alberta, with her family, where her three snoring dogs provide the soundtrack for her writing. For more information, visit alisonhughesbooks.com.

More messy adventures from neat freak Beatrice.